For Molly Elizabeth Davies
—*W. H. H.*

For Julio
—*V. L.*

The oral tradition of storytelling has deep roots in the lush
valleys and stony mountainsides of Appalachia. The original
European tales that the settlers brought with them centuries ago
have undergone continuous change in the telling and retelling
by local bards, who have adapted them bit by bit to fit a specific
locale and to hold spellbound a particular audience. In time the
classic folk- and fairy tales of European origin have evolved into
a distinctive body of oral literature that seems to have sprung
from the indigenous rocky soil of Appalachia.

Snowbear Whittington is based on the various oral versions
that I have heard over the years of what began as *Beauty and
the Beast*.   W. H. H.

*Library of Congress Cataloging-in-Publication Data. Hooks, William H. (retold by). Snowbear Whittington
/ William H. Hooks ; illustrated by Victoria Lisi. — 1st ed.   p.   cm. Summary: A tale about a girl
whose true love breaks a spell and turns her husband from a snow-white bear back into a handsome young
man. ISBN 0-02-744355-8 [1. Fairy tales. 2. Folklore—United States.] I. Lisi, Victoria, ill.
II. Title. PZ8.H77Sn 1994   398.21—dc20   93-8691*

Snowbear Whittington

An Appalachian Beauty and the Beast

William H. Hooks

Illustrated by Victoria Lisi

Macmillan Publishing Company   New York   Maxwell Macmillan Canada   Toronto
Maxwell Macmillan International   New York   Oxford   Singapore   Sydney

A long time ago,
in the mist-covered Smoky Mountains,
there lived a man with three daughters.
Nell, the youngest daughter,
kept their cabin bright and clean,
while Kate and Julia, the older daughters,
complained of the long, harsh winter
that kept them cabin bound.

When the snows began to melt,
  the father planned a trip to town.
"What shall I bring you, daughters?"
  he asked.

"New gowns!" shrieked Kate.
"Bring me a silken gown,
  the color of every bird that flies!"

Julia clapped her hands and cried,
"Bring me a silken gown, too,
  one the color of every flower
  on the mountain!"

Nell knew her father was too poor
  to buy silk gowns for all.
"If you should see a Christmas rose
  that still blooms in the melting snow,
  I would dearly love one," said Nell.

The father bought the silk dresses,
even though it meant less food.
On the way home, he searched
the mountainside for Christmas roses.
At dusk, as the mists began to gather,
he finally saw a patch
of the creamy white flowers.
He reached down to pluck one.
Suddenly a voice called out, "Break them not!"

The father was startled,
but he saw no one.
Often there were strange echoes
in the mountains.
He broke the largest rose,
and the voice cried again:

> *"Now you owe me,*
> *now sealed is your fate.*
> *Now you must give me*
> *what you meet at the gate."*

The old man hurried home
with the gifts for his daughters.
Who would want the old dog
that always met him at the gate?

It was dark
when the father reached the cabin.
And standing by the gate was Nell,
holding a candle to light his way.
"Go back, dear Nell," he called.

But Nell rushed forward
and hugged her father.
"You brought my rose!" she cried.

They hurried into the cabin.
While Kate and Julia
tried on their silk dresses,
her father told Nell
about the strange voice of the roses.
"I'm sure you imagined it,"
said Nell.

Just then there was a loud rapping
at the gate.
A voice called out:
> *"Now sealed is your fate.*
> *Now you must give me*
> *what you met at the gate."*

"Send out the dog.
  He'll chase it away," said Julia.
But the old dog whimpered
and hid behind the cabin.

The voice called again:
> *"Now sealed is your fate.*
> *Now you must give me*
> *what you met at the gate."*

"Come, Julia," said Kate.
"Two fine ladies in silk dresses
  can chase the beggar away."
  Out they marched into the night,
  and just as quickly they returned.
"There's a frightful beast out there!"
  Kate cried. "What can we do?"

"I must go," said Nell.
"It was I who asked for the rose."

N ell saw a great white bear,
fierce and menacing,
standing beside the gate.
"Climb on my back," said the beast.
"We've a journey to make."

Nell was terribly afraid
of the huge bear,
but she did as he commanded.
She rode the white bear's back
past the patch of Christmas roses,
over sharp and jagged rocks,
higher and higher into the mists
that shrouded the mountaintops.
Tears fell from her eyes,
and as they spilled onto the bear's back,
they turned to red stains,
like drops of her own heart's blood.

On the top of the highest peak,
Nell saw the heavy oak doors
of a stone house as large as a castle.

"Go inside," growled the beast,
"and light the candles."
The bear followed her in
and stood hidden in the shadows.

As Nell lighted the candles,
she was amazed to see such a splendid house.
But even more amazing,
before her eyes the ferocious bear
changed into a handsome young man.

"My name is Snowbear Whittington,"
  he said.
"This is your new home.
  There is a spell on me,
  cast by the Winter Witch
  to punish me for gathering snow roses
  that she claimed were hers alone.
  Now half of the time I must be a beast.
  Would you like me to be a bear
  by day or by night?"

  Nell hesitated a moment.
"I might truly fear a bear at night,
  so please be yourself by night,
  and we'll make the best we can
  of the day."

Soon Nell came to love
the handsome young man,
and her nights were happy.
But she dreaded the dawn of each day,
when Snowbear changed
into his ferocious bear self.
Nell begged Snowbear the man
to tell her how the witch's spell
could be broken.

"She only spoke a riddle," he said.
"It goes like this:
> *'When heart's blood*
> *spills on purest gold,*
> *the spell will lose*
> *its desperate hold.'*
I know not what it means,"
said Snowbear Whittington sadly.

Nell still missed her family.
One night she dreamed her father was ill.
The next morning she said to Snowbear,
"I must go to my father."

"No!" growled the beast.
"You may not go!"

Nell was surprised to see a look of hurt
on the beast's face.
She realized that even in the form of a beast
he had tender feelings,
and she felt sorry for him.

Nell pleaded with Snowbear the man.
Finally he agreed that she could go.
"But you must promise never to tell my name.
If you tell my name
the spell will become complete,
and after three days
I will remain a beast
by both night and day."

Nell promised, and Snowbear Whittington
carried her on his back
down from the highest mountain
to the gate of her father's house.
"Remember your promise," he said,
and loped off into the mists.

There was great joy in the little cabin.
Nell's father felt better
the moment he saw her.
Her sisters teased Nell.
"Tell us about your husband!"
Kate asked a dozen times a day.

"He must be rich to dress you
in such fine clothes," said Julia.

But Nell only laughed and said,
"My secrets are my secrets."

When her father was well,
  Nell spoke of returning.
"Put my heart at ease," said her father.
"Tell me the name of your husband."

It broke Nell's heart to see
the sorrowful look in her father's eyes.
Knowing that she could trust her father,
she whispered into his ear,
"Snowbear Whittington."

As the words died on her lips,
Nell heard a terrible groan,
like that of a wild animal caught in a trap.
She rushed outside.
Snowbear Whittington, the beast,
was groaning in pain.
He looked at her, gnashed his teeth,
and said, "You have broken your promise.
You have betrayed me!"
Then he ran howling up the mountain.
As the last rays of the sun disappeared,
Nell saw the red stains on his snowy back,
like heart's blood.

Nell went searching for Snowbear.
She soon lost her way
in the dark, fog-shrouded mountains.
As she cried out in despair,
a white bird flew by
and dropped a feather in her path.
Nell followed the bird
all through the night.
In the early morning it came to rest
at a tiny cabin deep in the woods.

An old, crippled woman
with long, white braids and a face
wrinkled and brown as a walnut
hobbled to the door.

"Have you seen a stranger pass
    through these parts?" asked Nell.

"Oh, yes," replied the old woman.
"A young man with red blood stains
    on the back of his shirt."

"When? Please tell me when!" cried Nell.
"Only the night just passed," said the old woman.

 Nell wanted to leave right away,
 but the old woman would not have it.
"Stay a day and a night," she ordered.

"But I must find him in three days!" cried Nell.

"Now listen," said the old woman.
"You be my hands for weaving,
    and I'll help you
    find your husband in time."

That morning they cleaned
and dyed the wool into bright colors.
The old woman gave Nell a pecan,
made from solid brass.

In the afternoon they spun
the colored wool into thread.
The old woman gave Nell a chestnut,
made from shiny silver.

That night they wove
the bright threads into a shawl
with all the colors of the rainbow.
The old woman gave Nell an acorn,
made from purest gold.

The next morning the old woman said,
"Go now, follow the white bird
to your husband, and remember,
use your three gifts only
when you are in grave trouble."

With the pecan, the chestnut, and the acorn
in her pocket, Nell struck out.
The white bird guided her
deeper and deeper into the mountains.

They came to a raging river,
and the bird flew to the other side.
Nell could find no way to cross over.
She remembered the old woman's words.
Quickly she cracked the brass pecan.
Out flew a hundred blackbirds.
They held a tree limb in their claws.
Nell grasped the limb,
and the birds flew her
safely across the raging river.

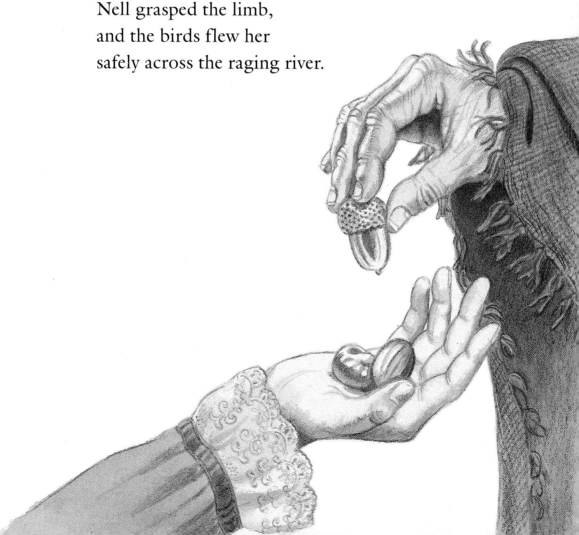

On and on she followed the white bird,
up a steep mountain peak
that rose into the clouds.
Night closed in.
Nell could no longer see the white bird
or the rocky path beneath her feet.
Any moment she might plunge to her death.
From her pocket she pulled the silver chestnut
and cracked it on a rock.
Thousands of fireflies burst out,
lighting her way through
the treacherous mountains.

All the next day the white bird
led Nell down from the high mountains,
into a fair green valley.
Nell grew fearful as night approached.
The third day of her search was ending,
and she had not found Snowbear.
As darkness fell around her,
a great weariness overtook her
and she fell asleep.

The frantic chirping of the white bird
awakened Nell.
She followed the bird
through the moon-drenched valley
to a stream.
There a group of young girls
were washing clothes.

Standing in the midst of the girls
was a man in a white shirt
with red stains on the back.
Hidden behind a tree, Nell watched.
"Help me!" cried the man.
"I'll marry the one who can wash
the stains from this shirt."

Quickly Nell covered her face
and got in line to wash the shirt.
But the girl before her
washed out the stains
and claimed Snowbear for her own.
Morning was fast approaching,
and Nell knew that Snowbear the man
would change forever into his bear shape.
She followed Snowbear and the girl
down the path to the girl's cabin.

Snowbear began to change,
but the girl paid no heed
until she reached the cabin door.
Then she turned and looked
into the face of the bear beast.

The girl screamed
as she fled inside the cabin.
Snowbear Whittington groaned
and fell to the ground.

Nell rushed to him.
She snatched the gold acorn
from her pocket,
hoping this last gift could save the beast.
"Dear one," she cried, "do not die.
I love you both as man and beast
with all my heart."
Her tears splashed down
onto the gold acorn,
staining it red as heart's blood.
The acorn cracked apart,
and Christmas roses poured out,
covering the great white bear.

Through Nell's head ran the words:

"When heart's blood
spills on purest gold,
the spell will lose
its desperate hold."

As she wept, the mound of roses
began to tremble,
and from the creamy blossoms
Snowbear Whittington the man arose.

He smiled at Nell
and took her in his arms.
"Your love has broken the spell,"
he said.
"Come, let's go home again."